mary-kateandashley

TWO of a kind ™

One Twin Too Many

D1389115

Look for these

TWO of a kind ™

titles:

1 *It's a Twin Thing*
2 *How to Flunk Your First Date*
3 *The Sleepover Secret*
4 *One Twin Too Many*

mary-kateandashley

TWO of a kind ™

One Twin Too Many

adapted by Megan Stine

from the teleplay by Howard Adler and Bob Griffard

from the series created by Robert Griffard
& Howard Adler

▥HarperCollins*Entertainment*
An Imprint of HarperCollins*Publishers*

A PARACHUTE PRESS BOOK

A PARACHUTE PRESS BOOK
Parachute Publishing, L.L.C.
156 Fifth Avenue
Suite 325
NEW YORK
NY 10010

First published in the USA by HarperEntertainment 1999
First published in Great Britain by Collins 2002
HarperCollins*Entertainment* is an imprint of HarperCollins*Publishers* Ltd,
77-85 Fulham Palace Road, Hammersmith, London W6 8JB

The HarperCollins website address is
www.fireandwater.com

6

ISBN 0 00 714477 6

Printed and bound in Great Britain by Clays Ltd, St Ives plc

CHAPTER
ONE

"Is he watching me?" Ashley Burke whispered to her twin sister, Mary-Kate. They stood in the doorway of Miss Tandy's seventh-grade classroom after lunch.

"Is who watching you?" Mary-Kate asked in a normal voice.

"Shh! Not so loud!" Ashley scolded her sister. "Don't let him hear you. Pokey Valentine – that's who!"

Mary-Kate rolled her eyes and tugged on her basketball jersey. "You've had a crush on him for a long time," she said.

"Yeah, tomorrow's our one-month anniversary," Ashley answered dreamily.

"Anniversary?" Mary-Kate said. "Since when? I didn't know you two were really a couple."

"We're not – yet," Ashley admitted. "But I've been *thinking* about going out with him for a whole month! Is he watching me?"

"No," Mary-Kate said. "He's trying to put a spitball down David Mouseman's shirt. Why?"

"I've got a mayonnaise stain on my dress," Ashley explained. "I don't want him to see it – so I've been waiting for the right moment to walk back to my seat."

Mary-Kate squinted hard at her sister's dress. Her eyes popped open in amazement.

"You're worried about a tiny little mayonnaise blop?" she asked. "It's the size of a pinhead!"

Ashley nodded. "Isn't it awful? I'm never bringing tuna salad for lunch again," she vowed. "It's ruining my life!"

"Well," Mary-Kate said, shaking her head, "I don't exactly think a guy with a *spitball* in his hands is going to be too grossed out by a mayo stain. But if you want to slip past him without being seen – this is your chance. Go for it!"

"Thanks!" Ashley said as she hurried to her seat.

As soon as Ashley sat down, Miss Tandy walked into the room.

"Class. Quiet down now, please," Miss Tandy began. "You'll have plenty of time to talk in just a little while – when you're done choosing partners for your history projects."

Partners? Ashley thought. *Did she say partners? As in working together? Side by side?*

I want Pokey! Ashley squeezed her lips shut tightly so she wouldn't blurt out the words.

Two rows behind Ashley, her friend Brian raised his hand.

"Why can't we have partners for the history test?" he called out.

Everyone laughed – except Miss Tandy.

"Brian – maybe you and I should be partners for the history test next week," Miss Tandy joked. "Would you like to sit right here, next to me, while you take it?"

Brian blushed and swallowed hard. "Uh – why?" he shot back. "Do you want to copy my answers?" Everyone laughed again. *Even* Miss Tandy.

"No, thank you, Brian," Miss Tandy answered. "Not after seeing the grade you got on your last test!"

Ashley turned around to check out Brian's face. He was laughing, too.

"Now, class, I've put all of your names on slips of

3

paper. And I've put half of the papers in this hat," Miss Tandy announced. She held up a black bowler hat that usually sat on a high shelf in the corner of the room. "But I need a second hat for the rest of the names. Mary-Kate?"

Ashley whirled around again, this time to check out her sister. Yes, she was wearing her baseball cap today. It was firmly planted – backwards – on her blonde head.

That's one of the ways that everyone at school can tell us apart, Ashley thought. *By how we dress.*

Mary-Kate was usually in jeans, sports jerseys or T-shirts, and a baseball cap.

Ashley dressed in every cool outfit she could lay her hands on. Clothes were Ashley's thing.

"Do you want my cap?" Mary-Kate asked.

"Just for a moment, if you please," Miss Tandy replied.

"Sure." Mary-Kate nodded, taking her hat up to the front of the classroom.

Ashley held her breath, wondering if Mary-Kate would absolutely die of embarrassment when people saw how squashed flat her hair was from wearing the hat all day.

Nope! Ashley realised. Her sister didn't care about bad hair at all!

4

Ashley fixed one of the hair clips in her own blonde hair – just to make it more perfect.

Miss Tandy smiled a thank-you at Mary-Kate. Then she dumped the second pile of names into the baseball cap.

"All right, class," Miss Tandy announced. "Here we go!"

Without looking down, she plunged one hand into the black bowler and pulled out a name. She stuck her other hand into Mary-Kate's hat and pulled out another name.

"Here are the first two partners for the history project," Miss Tandy announced. "Alicia Alston, your partner is . . . Jessica Reich! All right, girls. You may get together quietly, in the back of the room, and begin deciding what you want to do for your project.

"And the next pair of names is . . . "

Ashley and Pokey! Ashley silently prayed.

Ashley and Pokey. Ashley and Pokey. Ashley and Pokey.

She said it over and over in her head – like a chant.

It sounded so *good*.

If I wish hard enough, Ashley thought . . .

"Pokey Valentine and . . . " Miss Tandy plunged

her hand into the other hat. "Mary-Kate Burke."

What? Ashley felt her face getting hot. That couldn't be right. What was Miss Tandy trying to do? Break up a beautiful relationship – before it even got off the ground?

But tomorrow's our one-month anniversary! Ashley almost blurted out.

Ashley glanced back at Mary-Kate, who simply shrugged.

It's a mistake, Ashley thought. But she didn't know what to do about it. Miss Tandy began calling out other names.

And then Ashley heard her own name.

"Ashley Burke and . . . "

Miss Tandy took a slip of paper out of the other hat.

"David Mouseman."

Ew! Ashley thought. *Yuck!* How could she possibly do a history project with *him?* David Mouseman was so – so *un*cool. He had thick glasses and greasy hair. He had a spitball down his back – and he probably didn't even know it yet!

A moment later David appeared in front of Ashley's seat.

"Hi," he mumbled. "I, uh, guess we'll be working together. What do you want to do our project on? I was thinking of a forty-page research paper on the Gettysburg Address."

"I had a different address in mind," Ashley mumbled under her breath. "Pokey Valentine's address!"

"What?" David Mouseman asked.

"Uh, nothing," Ashley replied glumly. She stared across the room, toward the windows. Mary-Kate and Pokey were hanging out, talking about something.

If Ashley knew her sister, they *weren't* talking about the history project. Mary-Kate didn't worry too much about grades or school. And she could care less who she did her project with. They were probably talking about basketball.

Suddenly Ashley had an idea.

A brilliant idea.

"Wait right here," she told David. She gripped him by the shoulders and forced him to sit down in her seat.

Then she dashed across the crowded classroom. She headed straight for her sister.

"Mary-Kate," Ashley said, interrupting Mary-Kate and Pokey's conversation. "Can I see you for a minute? Privately? I, uh, need to borrow something from you."

"Sure," Mary-Kate agreed. She followed her sister to a corner of the room. "What do you want to borrow?"

"Your partner," Ashley answered softly. "I want Pokey Valentine!"

CHAPTER TWO

"Oh, no. I'm not lending you Pokey Valentine. No way," Mary-Kate declared, shaking her head. She crossed her arms firmly over her chest.

"Why not?" Ashley pleaded.

"Why should I?" Mary-Kate argued. "He's already got a good idea for the history project – and he doesn't care if he has to do most of the work."

"Come on," Ashley begged. "You know how much I like him. And you're my sister! You've got to make a deal with me! You've got to let me borrow him."

Mary-Kate thought for a minute.

"Okay, we can make a deal," she agreed with a small smile. "But 'borrow' isn't the word I'd use."

"What is the word?" Ashley asked.

"'Buy'!" Mary-Kate declared. "If you want Pokey Valentine, you're going to have to pay for him – big time!"

Ashley didn't even bother asking Mary-Kate how much. Whatever it was – it was going to be worth it. "No problem," Ashley said. "Wait right here. I'll get my wallet."

But before she could make her way toward her seat, Miss Tandy was calling the class to order.

"Class, you have five more minutes for discussion," Miss Tandy announced. "Then we'll have to move on to maths review."

Ashley changed direction quickly.

"Only five minutes left to be alone with Pokey!" she announced to her sister. "I'll pay you later." Then she added, "Oh, by the way, David Mouseman is waiting for you – in my seat!"

Ashley zoomed over to the windows as fast as she could. She put on her sweetest smile.

"Hi, Pokey," she said. "Uh, there's been a change in plans. Mary-Kate and I had to switch partners for the history project because of . . . uh . . . because of her basketball schedule."

"Huh?" Pokey looked confused. "I don't get it. Why does her basketball schedule have anything to do with the history project?"

Don't make this hard for me! Ashley thought.

"Who knows?" Ashley muttered. "You'll have to ask *her* about that. Anyway, since we're sisters, I was *more* than happy to help her out!"

"Okay," Pokey agreed. "What do you want to do for our project?"

"I don't know," Ashley replied, staring dreamily at his light brown hair.

Right now, I can't think of a thing! Ashley realised. *I can't remember a single historical event.*

I can't even remember who won the Revolutionary War!

"Uh . . . do you have any ideas?" she finally managed to ask.

"Yeah," Pokey nodded. "I was sort of thinking of something to do with Lewis and Clark, the explorers."

A famous historical twosome? Ashley thought. She liked the sound of that.

"Great!" Ashley agreed quickly. "Two people who made history – *together.* I like the way you think!"

"I am so brilliant!" Ashley announced as she and Mary-Kate waltzed in the door after school that day. Carrie, the twins' twenty-six-year-old babysitter, glanced up from the textbook she was reading.

Carrie was a student in a science class that the twins' father taught at college. That's how Kevin Burke met Carrie. Mary-Kate and Ashley convinced their father to hire her as their babysitter soon after that.

Ever since the twins' mother died three years ago, Kevin needed someone to be there when the girls came home from school. Carrie was their best babysitter so far. She helped Mary-Kate with her jump shot – and Ashley with her clothes. They both loved having her around.

"Okay, I'll bite," Carrie said. "Tell us, Ashley. Why are you so brilliant this time?"

"Because," Ashley explained, "when Miss Tandy assigned partners for our history project, I made sure I got teamed up with Pokey Valentine!"

Carrie raised her eyebrows. "Wow!" she exclaimed. "How did you manage that?"

"She paid his *first* partner to trade with her," Mary-Kate answered.

"Smart," Carrie said. "How much?"

Mary-Kate pulled a bill out of her jeans pocket and waved it around.

"Ten bucks!" she announced triumphantly.

"Not bad." Not bad at all. Carrie closed her

textbook and tossed it aside on the couch.

"Hmmm," she muttered thoughtfully. "Maybe I should try that. There's a cute guy in your dad's class I'd love to spend some time with. I wonder who his lab partner is."

Cute? Ashley thought. *I bet he's not as cute as Pokey!*

Ashley danced around the living room dreamily, clutching her backpack in her arms. But in her mind, it wasn't a backpack at all. She was actually dancing with Pokey Valentine.

Carrie smiled at her. "You've had a crush on Pokey for a long time, haven't you?" she commented.

"Yeah," Mary-Kate answered sarcastically. "Tomorrow's their one-month anniversary. Of course, she'll be the only one celebrating – because Pokey has no idea he's in a relationship!"

"Most men don't," Carrie joked. "So Ashley, what are you making for your project?"

"A map tracing the Lewis and Clark expedition," Ashley announced proudly.

Carrie nodded. "I like it!" she said, sounding impressed. "And what are you making, Mary-Kate?"

"How should I know?" Mary-Kate snapped. "It's

not even due till next week!"

I wish it weren't due till next year! Ashley thought.
*Then Pokey and I could work on this project together
for months and months!*

CHAPTER THREE

"So it's safe to conclude that the worst damage to the ozone layer is over the South Pole," Kevin Burke told his college class the next afternoon.

He paced in front of the classroom wearing his standard tweed jacket, crisp blue shirt, and striped tie.

Carrie sat in the front row, taking notes. She wore black boots, bright green stretch jeans, and a wild paisley print shirt, not tucked in.

Her full red hair was clipped in six different places at once. But one piece flopped over her eyes, hiding them. It allowed her to peek sideways without being seen.

She glanced back to her left and got a fix on the

supercute guy in the second row. The one who was her new lab partner. His name was Rick.

He looks just like a Rick, Carrie decided. *Strong. Muscular. Great hair. Confident voice.*

She loved the way his grey athletic jersey made him look like a hunk and his tortoiseshell glasses made him look supersmart at the same time.

He must be a grad student, she decided. He had to be, since he was a little older than most of the other people in the class. Or maybe he took time off from college, just the way she had.

Rick had asked for her phone number right before class. *If he calls me, I'll find out,* she thought.

"Excuse me, Professor," Rick said, interrupting.

"Again?" Professor Burke said. He sounded frustrated.

No wonder, Carrie thought. It *was* the fifth time Rick had interrupted Professor Burke that day. But why shouldn't he – if he had something important to say?

"If I may," Rick said.

Professor Burke nodded – grudgingly.

"I recently read a piece in *Time* magazine," Rick began, "which contradicts your entire argument."

Professor Burke didn't flinch.

"You know, Rick," Kevin answered, "I pretty

much lost faith in *Time* magazine when they put down one of my favourite movies – *The Nutty Professor.*"

Everyone else in the class laughed.

"Now, an ozone dent has also appeared over the northern part of the globe," Professor Burke went on.

But Rick interrupted him again.

"Excuse me, Professor," he said, not waiting for a go-ahead, "but a lot of people think that global warming is just something the media is making up. That there isn't much truth to it."

He is so smart, Carrie thought, staring at Rick. And so totally confident-sounding. She wished she had the nerve to argue with her professors that way.

"Really?" Professor Burke shot back. "Well, to anyone who thinks that the ozone problem isn't real – I recommend a very good sunscreen!"

Okay – that was funny, Carrie decided. But why did Professor Burke have to make fun of *everything* Rick said?

"Professor," Carrie called out, "you still haven't answered Rick's point. Which I think is a good one."

"Thank you," Rick said, shooting Carrie a fabulous smile.

17

Those eyes! Carrie thought.

"My pleasure," she said in her most admiring tone of voice.

Kevin Burke cleared his throat at the front of the class. "I'd be happy to address that point," he said. He sounded totally in charge and sure of himself. "The latest satellite photos show that the ozone damage is far *worse* than anyone thought. And you can find those photos in the *Journal of Earth Science* – which, by the way, loved *The Nutty Professor*!"

Everyone around Carrie laughed at the professor's joke.

Professor Burke glanced at his watch.

"All right, class is over," he announced. "So get out of here. We'll continue this next time."

The students shuffled out of the room. But Carrie took her time, as usual. She liked to hang back, just in case Professor Burke had something he wanted to tell her about babysitting for the girls.

And, as usual, he did.

"Oh, Carrie, I'll be home a little early this afternoon," Kevin said. "Ashley's starting her history project today, and I want to get a peek at this Pokey Valentine."

Carrie nodded. "I don't blame you," she agreed.

"After hearing about him for a whole month, I'm kind of curious myself. Hey, that was a great lecture today, by the way."

"Apparently Rick didn't think so," Professor Burke complained.

"He gets on your nerves, doesn't he?" Carrie asked.

Kevin Burke sighed. "Every term somebody always does. At first this year I thought it was going to be *you* – but today Rick pulled ahead."

"Thanks, I guess!" Carrie mumbled. "Well, I think Rick's kind of cute."

Kevin rolled his eyes. "Are you kidding? You like him?"

"I guess so." Carrie nodded. "I mean, I gave him my phone number."

Kevin shrugged. "Well, in that case, I have nothing further to say."

Carrie wrapped her arms around her books and headed for the door.

"Except, Carrie . . . how did you manage to end up with Rick as a lab partner, anyway?" Kevin called after her.

How? Carrie thought. *Oh, just a little trick I learned from your daughter…* Yesterday, Carrie had paid Rick's first lab partner to switch with her!

"How? Oh, that's for me to know – and you to wonder about!" Carrie replied with a laugh and a twinkle in her eyes.

Then she hurried out the door before Kevin could quiz her more.

Yeah, Carrie thought. *Thanks to Ashley, Rick and I will be working together – for months and months!*

CHAPTER FOUR

"So how do I look?" Ashley asked nervously. "Pokey's going to be here any minute – I've got to be ready!"

Ashley stood in the middle of the living room wearing her newest outfit – a blue slip dress, with blue lace edging at the top. She wore a little blue cardigan sweater over it, to match.

"You're not wearing *that* dress, are you?" Mary-Kate exclaimed, making a face.

"I knew it! It makes me look dumpy, doesn't it?" Ashley worried out loud. Instantly she turned to run back upstairs.

"No! Don't try anything else on!" Mary-Kate exclaimed. She turned to Carrie. "Our room already looks like an explosion at the mall – and all the clothing fallout landed on us!"

"Whoa, Ashley!" Carrie called. "Hold on! You look perfect."

"Really?" Ashley asked. Her voice cracked.

I mean, I've got to look perfect! Ashley thought. *Or Pokey might not get the message. The message that he and I are meant for each other!*

"Yes," Carrie reassured her. "You look great. Honestly."

"You don't look that bad," Mary-Kate chimed in. "If you like all that lacy stuff," she mumbled.

Carrie narrowed her eyes at Mary-Kate. "Way to be supportive, Mary-Kate," she said.

Ashley glanced at the clock on the mantel and began pacing nervously around the living room.

"Did you get the Double Fudge Crunch Bars?" she asked Carrie. "Because I told you – Pokey loves those."

"They're in the kitchen," Carrie answered in a soothing voice. "Stay cool – I hear someone outside."

Ashley's head snapped toward the door as the doorbell rang.

"I've got it!" she whispered loudly, just to make

absolutely sure that Mary-Kate wouldn't rush over and answer it.

She took a deep breath, put on her most glowing smile, and walked to the front door. Then she flung it open.

Oh, wow, Ashley thought, the minute she set eyes on Pokey Valentine.

Pokey stood there with his sandy-brown hair falling over his eyes. He had his schoolbooks under one arm, and a skateboard under the other. He was wearing a green-and-navy crew shirt, jeans, and white basketball shoes with the laces half-undone.

Ashley couldn't decide whether the thing with the laces was an out-of-date fashion statement, or a mistake.

But either way, she didn't care! He was adorable.

"Hi, Ashley," Pokey Valentine said, sounding a bit nervous himself.

"Hi, Pokey," Ashley almost cooed. She moved aside so he could come in.

What now? she thought. *How come when I finally get him alone I can't think of a thing to say?*

She glanced quickly at Carrie and Mary-Kate, who were hanging around.

"Hi, Pokey. I'm Carrie," the babysitter said in her most friendly and welcoming tone of voice. "I've

23

heard a lot about you."

Whoa! Ashley thought. *Don't go there, Carrie! I don't want him thinking I talk about him all the time or anything!*

At least not until I find out if he likes me.

"You've heard a lot about me?" Pokey repeated, puzzled. "From who?"

Ashley shot Carrie a warning glance. *Careful, Carrie!* she silently prayed.

Carrie cleared her throat. "Uh, well, not about you, uh, *personally,*" she corrected herself. "But I did hear about the history project – so, naturally, your name came up. You know, Lewis . . . Clark . . . Pokey. Right?"

Phew! Close one! Ashley let out a tiny sigh of relief. She shot Carrie a grateful smile. Carrie was cool that way. She was good at covering up all sorts of things.

"I'm going to go shoot some hoops," Mary-Kate announced. She hopped off the couch and headed for the door. "Bye, Ashley. See ya, Porky."

"It's *Pokey,*" Ashley snapped at her sister.

"Whatever." Mary-Kate shrugged on her way out.

That takes care of one of them, Ashley thought. *Now there's just Carrie…*

Ashley was feeling pretty nervous about this date, even though it wasn't a real date at all. She didn't know whether she wanted Carrie to go – or stay.

Ashley glanced at Carrie and gulped. Then she looked at Pokey. She couldn't think of a thing to say. The silence was killing her.

Her heart started pounding.

Say something! she told herself.

"So, uh . . . you want a soda?" she asked Pokey.

"Sure," he agreed.

Good! Ashley thought. *At least this gives me something to do!*

Nervously she dashed out of the living room to the kitchen – leaving Carrie with the job of making conversation!

In the kitchen Ashley hunted for some nice glasses to serve the soda in. But nothing was clean. Finally she spotted two tall blue glasses sitting in the dishwasher.

I'll wash those, Ashley decided.

But first, she peeked into the living room to see how things were going.

Carrie had kicked off her shoes and put her feet up on the sofa.

"Nice skateboard," Carrie said to Pokey, eyeing

the equipment under his arm.

"Thanks," Pokey answered.

Carrie cocked her head sideways to read the brand name. "Hey, Pig Wheels!" she said enthusiastically. "You know, I'm thinking of getting a set. I hear they're good with curbs. How do they handle rails? Are you happy with the grip?"

Pokey shrugged. A helpless expression spread across his face. "Hey – I don't know, lady," he answered. "I just ride the thing to look cool!"

Oh, man, Ashley thought. *She's making him even more nervous than I am!*

Ashley heard her father's car pull up in the driveway.

Uh-oh, she thought. *I'd better get out there fast, before Dad comes in!*

But she was curious about what her father would say when he met Pokey. She heard Kevin come in through the front door.

He was slightly out of breath.

"Hi, Carrie!" he said as he dropped his briefcase. Then Ashley heard him whisper, "Am I in time?"

In time for what? Ashley wondered. She peeked into the living room and saw Carrie nodding toward Pokey.

"Oh! I see we have company," Kevin Burke said.

"Yes, Professor." Carrie introduced them. "This is Pokey Valentine."

Pokey stood up to shake hands.

"Hi, Pokey. I'm Ashley's father."

"Hi," Pokey grunted.

"That's quite a handshake you've got there," Kevin said.

"I work out," Pokey announced with a proud grin.

"Well, have a seat," Kevin offered, pointing to the couch.

I should go in now, Ashley thought. She hopped nervously up and down. *Before Dad sits Pokey down and starts grilling him like he's a criminal or something!*

Ashley darted to the refrigerator to get the soda. From the kitchen she overheard her dad asking Pokey about his name.

"It's kind of an unusual name," Kevin commented. "How did you get it?"

"I have weird parents," Pokey replied. "They thought it would be cute to name their kids after the Seven Dwarfs."

"Uh . . . Pokey's not one of the Seven Dwarfs," Kevin pointed out.

"Neither is Prancer," Pokey shot back.

"Who's Prancer?" Kevin asked, confused.

"That's my sister," Pokey announced flatly.

Okay, that's it, Ashley thought.

She pushed open the kitchen door and hurried in with the two tall blue glasses full of soda.

"Hi, Dad," she greeted her father quickly. "Here's our soda, Pokey. Excuse us, Dad, but we've really got to get started on our project, if you know what I mean."

"But Pokey and I were having a nice chat," Kevin complained.

Ashley shot Carrie a pleading glance. *Bail me out, here*, she thought. *Please, Carrie!*

Carrie quickly took Kevin by the arm.

"Why don't we get out of here so these guys can work quietly?" she suggested.

Thank you, Carrie! Ashley thought.

As soon as they were gone, Ashley turned to Pokey.

"Well, should we get busy?" she asked. She gestured towards the coffee table where they were going to work. "Or can I get you something to eat to go along with these sodas? Crisps, maybe? Or popcorn? Or my personal favourite, Double Fudge Crunch Bars!"

"Double Fudge Crunch Bars?" Pokey looked amazed. "I love those, too!"

"Wow! What a coincidence!" Ashley exclaimed, pretending to be totally surprised.

She smiled to herself. *It pays to do research!* she thought.

Ashley let out a sigh and began to relax. *Okay*, she decided. This was a good start.

And if she could just keep her dad and Carrie out of the way, maybe she and Pokey would actually get a chance to talk to each other. Alone.

Now she had only one problem left.

All Ashley needed was . . . to think of something else to say!

CHAPTER FIVE

"Okay, Professor, I'm finished here," Carrie reported the next evening. "The girls are doing their homework, I'm going bowling, and you're out of diet root beer."

Kevin Burke looked up from the test paper he was grading.

"Diet root beer?" he asked. "Who drinks diet root beer?"

"I do," Carrie said.

"Then wouldn't that mean *you're* out of diet root beer?" he corrected her.

Carrie rolled her eyes. "What a job – the little extras just keep coming!"

Carrie wasn't really complaining. So far, this job

with the professor was working out really well.

She liked him. She *loved* the girls. And the money was just what she needed.

"Okay." She moved toward the door. "See you tomorrow."

But Kevin held up a finger.

"Uh, Carrie!" he said, as if he just remembered. "I was wondering . . . would you like to make some extra money this weekend?"

"Sure," Carrie answered quickly. "Why not? Especially now that I have to pay for my own root beer!"

"Good," Kevin said. "I need someone to watch the girls Saturday night. I'm going to the hockey game with Eddie."

Saturday night? No way! Carrie thought. She already had big plans for Saturday night.

"Oh, sorry, can't do it," she answered. "I'm going to the symphony with Rick."

Kevin dropped his pencil loudly.

"Rick?" he snapped. "You mean, Mr. Let's-interrupt-the-class-to-get-attention Rick? That Rick?"

"That's the guy!" Carrie agreed cheerfully.

Kevin shook his head.

"I don't get it," he muttered. "He doesn't seem like your type."

"Oh, really!" Carrie couldn't believe this! "Well, Professor, now that you've known me for a couple of weeks, what do you think my type is?"

Kevin thought about it for a minute.

"Oh, I don't know. An artist, maybe," he guessed. "Or a musician. Or an out-of-work housepainter, for all I know. Just not Rick."

Carrie crossed her arms and flipped a strand of red hair out of her face.

"I think I know why you don't like him," she said coolly.

"Because he's a conceited know-it-all who's in love with his own voice?" Kevin answered.

Carrie glared. "No."

"Boy, I thought for sure that was it!" Kevin shot back.

She pointed her finger at Kevin and tried not to lose her temper.

"You don't like Rick because he's got a mind of his own," Carrie accused Kevin. "He doesn't just go along with everything you say because you're the professor. He argues with you. And I think you feel threatened by that."

"That is the most ridiculous . . . !" Kevin started to argue. But then he stopped himself and shook his head. He seemed to be trying to stay calm.

"Never mind," he said.

"Aha!" Carrie gloated. "I touched a nerve there, didn't I?"

Kevin shook his head. "No. It's not that," he said in a softer tone. "It's just that I realised I shouldn't be giving you advice about whom to date. That's not my place. Your personal life is none of my business."

"Thank you!" Carrie blurted out. That was exactly what she had been thinking! "And your personal life is none of my business," she added.

"Exactly," Kevin agreed. "You should date Rick all you want. As long as I don't have to see him outside of class, I'm perfectly fine."

Just then the doorbell rang.

Uh-oh, Carrie thought. *If Professor Burke doesn't want to see Rick outside of class . . . he isn't going to like this!*

"I'll get it," she offered. She lunged for the door.

Kevin stood up anyway.

"Carrie, I can get it. It's my house," Kevin insisted.

"Yes," Carrie said, cutting in front of him quickly. "But it's my Rick!"

She flung open the door – and there he was. All six-foot-three of him! He was wearing a fuzzy brown sweater that made him look even cuter – and more huggable – than a teddy bear.

"Oh, hi, Profess— " Rick started to say.

But Carrie didn't let him get it out. She put a hand on his chest and pushed him. Backwards.

"Let's just go, okay?" she said. She wanted to get him out of the house before things turned ugly.

Boy, oh, boy, she thought, as she and Rick walked into the cool night air.

It was one thing to *talk* about keeping her private life and the professor's separate.

But it was another thing to actually *do* it!

CHAPTER SIX

"Boy, Lewis and Clark sure got around," Pokey moaned.

He and Ashley were sitting on their knees in the living room the next afternoon, bent over the coffee table. Their map of the Lewis and Clark expedition was spread out in front of them. Pokey was painting the left side of the map. Ashley was painting the right side.

"I'm amazed that they didn't get lost!" Ashley exclaimed.

"That's because they had a Native American guide, named Sacajawea," Pokey explained. "She knew the area and she was their guide for the whole trip."

"Sacajawea. That sure is a weird name!" Ashley said.

"If you want a weird name, try living with 'Pokey' for a while!" Pokey joked.

Ashley laughed and agreed. Pokey was a pretty strange name. But she didn't care what his name was! She liked him anyway.

This is the best, Ashley thought. *Working on the history project together. It's a perfect excuse to be with Pokey – alone – every single day until the map is done.*

Paint more slowly, she told herself. *That way you won't finish your part of the map too soon. And maybe we'll have to work together on Saturday, too!*

Pokey sat back on his heels and yawned. "I'm getting painter's cramp," he moaned. He shook his hand.

"Me, too," Ashley agreed. "We need a break. Do you want something to drink?"

"Yeah." Pokey nodded. "Do you know how to make a smoothie?"

A smoothie? Yikes! Ashley thought. She had absolutely no idea how to make a smoothie!

But she couldn't let Pokey know that.

"Are you kidding?" Ashley said. "*I* put the 'smooth' in smoothie! Pokey, you have *so much* to learn about me."

She jumped up and raced for the kitchen.

Carrie was sitting at the kitchen table, drinking a cup of tea. Ashley grabbed her by the shoulders.

"Carrie – quick! Do you know how to make a smoothie?" Ashley begged.

"Sure, why?" Carrie asked.

"Because I told Pokey I'd make him one, and I don't have a clue how to!" Ashley confessed.

Carrie twisted her mouth into a frown.

"So you lied to a boy just to impress him?" Carrie asked.

Ashley nodded. "Is that a bad thing?"

"Yes," Carrie admitted matter-of-factly. "But we all do it. You get the ice and strawberries. I'll get the blender."

"Thanks!" Ashley said, shooting her a smile. "You've saved my life."

"No problem," Carrie said, smiling back.

Ashley opened the refrigerator and peered inside. There was a basket of strawberries in the vegetable bin. She pulled it out and frowned.

Half of them were soft and mushy, starting to go bad.

"Oh, no. We're going to have to cut out these mouldy parts," Ashley moaned.

"So? What's the big problem?" Carrie asked.

"I'm just afraid it will take too long," Ashley explained. "I mean, every time Pokey comes over, I leave him sitting in the living room. And he gets stuck talking to someone else."

"You mean like the other day, when he got stuck talking to me?" Carrie asked.

Ashley shook her head fast. "No, that was okay. At least you didn't quiz him about all his family members. Or make him feel weird about having a strange name, the way Dad did."

"Well, there's no one in the living room to quiz him now," Carrie commented.

"I know," Ashley moaned. "That's even worse! I'm afraid he'll get bored and go home!"

Carrie glanced out of the window.

"Don't worry," she said. "Here comes Mary-Kate. Max and Brian are with her. They'll keep Pokey company while you're making the smoothie."

Max and Brian? Uh-oh. Ashley didn't like the sound of that. Who knew what they would say to him!

"That's even worse," Ashley said.

"What do you mean?" Carrie asked.

"I mean, what if Mary-Kate told them I like Pokey?" Ashley explained. "What if they blurt it out? Or what if they start teasing him about me? It could be a disaster in there."

Ashley cut the bad parts out of the strawberries as fast as she could.

"Relax, Ashley," Carrie said. "Your sister won't let anything like that happen. She knows Pokey is the man of your dreams."

Yeah, Ashley thought. *I guess that's true.*

At least Mary-Kate wouldn't let anything happen on *purpose*.

But how could she stop Max and Brian if they got started?

"It sure is hard having a boyfriend around here," Ashley muttered as she tossed the strawberries into the blender.

"You can say that again!" Carrie agreed with a big laugh.

CHAPTER SEVEN

"Oh, quit complaining," Mary-Kate grumbled as she, Max, and Brian walked in the front door. "I beat you fair and square."

"You always beat us fair and square!" Brian complained.

"And it's always bad. Very bad," Max moaned.

"And it always will be, until you find a way to stop my turnaround jump shot," Mary-Kate gloated. She twirled the basketball in her hand. "Which, by the way, is unstoppable."

Mary-Kate started to dribble the basketball on the living-room floor. But then she noticed Pokey sitting beside the coffee table. He was carefully painting the Lewis and Clark map.

40

Mary-Kate caught the ball before it bounced on the map.

"Hi, Mary-Kate," Pokey said, glancing up. "Hi, guys."

"Hey, Pokey," Max and Brian both said.

"Where's Ashley?" Mary-Kate asked. She flipped the basketball from one hand to another.

"She's in the kitchen, making me a smoothie," Pokey answered.

A smoothie? Mary-Kate thought. *Since when does Ashley know how to make a smoothie? Why hasn't she ever made one for me?*

"So, how's the map going?" Mary-Kate asked, still tossing the basketball.

"It's okay," Pokey answered with a shrug.

Then he put his paintbrush down and stood up. "Listen, Mary-Kate, are you doing anything Saturday?" he asked.

Huh?

Mary-Kate stopped flipping the ball. She set it down on the couch.

"Why?" she asked.

"I thought maybe you could come over to my house," Pokey explained. "You know – play basketball and stuff."

I don't really want to play basketball with Pokey,

Mary-Kate thought. *He's not even as good as Max or Brian.*

"Nah, I don't think so," she answered. She headed toward the dining room.

"I've got a fibreglass backboard," Pokey called after her.

Mary-Kate spun around.

Pokey had a fibreglass backboard? Those were the best!

"I'll be there at eleven!" she agreed quickly.

Just then the kitchen door swung open. Ashley stuck her head in.

"Pokey – your smoothie's ready!" she called proudly. "Let's drink them out here."

"Cool," Pokey said, tromping across the room.

Ashley disappeared back into the kitchen. But Pokey hung back for a minute.

"So I'll see you Saturday, Mary-Kate," he said over his shoulder.

Mary-Kate nodded. Then Pokey followed Ashley into the kitchen and the door swung shut.

"Whoa!" Max said. He shook his head at Mary-Kate. "Boy, have you got a problem!"

"Yeah," Brian chimed in. "A big problem!"

"What in the world are you talking about?" Mary-Kate asked.

"The guy your sister has the hots for just invited you out on a date," Max explained.

"No way!" Mary-Kate argued. "A date? That's ridiculous! He asked me over to play basketball – that's all."

"And stuff," Max added. "He said 'play basketball and stuff'. Remember?"

Mary-Kate felt her face getting hot. "You guys are crazy," she snapped. "Pokey was just— "

"Hey, trust me," Max interrupted her. "The 'and stuff' part makes it a date. Am I right, Brian?"

Brian shrugged. "Yeah, I guess so."

"But . . . " Mary-Kate tried to argue.

But she couldn't really think of anything else to say.

"Come on, Brian," Max said. He motioned towards the door. "Let's get out of here."

Brian shook his head at Mary-Kate.

"Boy – stealing your sister's boyfriend. That's the lowest!" he said. "I'm really disappointed in you, Mary-Kate."

Hold on! Mary-Kate wanted to say. *I never stole Ashley's boyfriend! At least . . . I didn't mean to!*

But it was too late. Max and Brian had already walked out of the house.

This isn't happening, Mary-Kate thought.

43

It wasn't a date – was it?

Because if it was, she knew Max and Brian were right.

She *was* in big trouble!

CHAPTER EIGHT

"Dad! Put that phone down – please! You have to stay off for the next half an hour," Ashley scolded her father. "Pokey's supposed to call me."

Kevin Burke sighed. But he did as his daughter asked. He put the phone down.

Kevin's best friend, Eddie, glanced up from the football game he was watching on TV.

"Pokey? Who's Pokey?" Eddie asked.

"Oh, he's just a boy I'm doing a history project with," Ashley answered. "No one special." She pressed her fingers into her dad's arm. "Half an hour, okay? Stay off the phone!"

"Got it." Kevin nodded.

"And don't pick it up if it rings!" Ashley reminded

him as she headed for the kitchen.

"Hmmm," Eddie said when Ashley was gone. "Either there's a cash prize for this history project, or somebody's in *love*."

Kevin laughed. "It's just a crush," he declared. "I met him yesterday. He's a nice twelve-year-old boy."

"Yeah, right," Eddie snapped. "Just like we were nice twelve-year-old boys . . . remember?"

"Don't start with me, Eddie," Kevin warned.

Who needs this? Kevin thought. *I have enough on my mind without worrying about Ashley and Pokey Valentine!*

He had tons of papers to grade before Monday, and time was running out.

Kevin turned back to the student paper he had been grading before Ashley came in. There was something oddly familiar about this report . . .

Oh, no.

His mouth slowly dropped open.

"I don't believe this!" Kevin said. He jumped up, raced to a bookcase in the living room, and pulled an old textbook off the shelf.

"What?" Eddie asked. "A paper with no spelling errors?"

Kevin shook his head. He began flipping through

the textbook until he found the right page. He stood with his head bowed, reading and mumbling for a minute.

"I knew it!" he finally announced.

"Knew what?" Eddie asked.

"Remember that guy Rick I told you about? The one who's going out with Carrie?" Kevin asked.

Eddie nodded. "You mean Mr. Know-it-all? Yeah, what about him?"

"He stole his entire paper from this book!" Kevin declared.

"Whoa!" Eddie whistled. "When I took the tests to get my plumber's licence, that was considered a no-no."

"Yeah, well, it's kind of frowned upon in college, too," Kevin snapped.

"Well, look on the bright side," Eddie advised. "You get to tell Carrie her boyfriend's a cheat! That'll be fun, won't it?"

"No way." Kevin shook his head. "I can't do that. Carrie and I made a deal that we'd stay out of each other's private lives. Besides, as a professor, I can't discuss one student's grade with another student. It wouldn't be right."

"Well, as a plumber, I live by no such rules," Eddie said, reaching for the phone. "What's Carrie's number?"

Kevin started to shake his head again. No way. He couldn't let Eddie do it.

But he didn't get a chance to say a word. Because Ashley yelled at both of them from the kitchen.

"Put down the phone!" she called.

"Okay, okay!" Eddie said, giving up. He placed the receiver back on the hook. "But you're going to have to deal with this *sometime*," he warned Kevin.

Yeah, Kevin thought, *I am*. Even if he didn't tell Carrie that her new boyfriend was a cheat – she was going to find out that something was wrong.

She'd find out when Rick got an F on his research paper!

And when that happened, Kevin had the sinking feeling that she was going to be really upset.

But not at Rick. At *him*!

CHAPTER NINE

"I'll show you," Mary-Kate said to Brian and Max the next day at school. The three of them were eating lunch in the cafeteria. "Pokey Valentine did not ask me out on a date. And I'm going to prove he didn't."

"How?" Max asked. He crossed his arms over his chest.

"Easy," Mary-Kate explained. "I'm going to . . . uh, go right up to him and ask him."

Brian slurped up a strand of spaghetti and laughed at the same time. Spaghetti sauce dripped out of his mouth.

"Let me get this straight," Brian said, still chewing. "You're going to go up to Pokey and say:

'Did you ask me for a date on Saturday?' "

"Right." Mary-Kate nodded. "What's wrong with that?"

"What if he says no?" Brian answered. "Then he'll think you were *hoping* it was a date – even if it wasn't. He'll think you're after him. You'll be humiliated."

Oh, no! Mary-Kate thought. *He's right!*

That was the last thing in the world she wanted. It would be awful if Pokey thought she was chasing after him.

Mary-Kate wasn't going to chase after any guy. Ever.

She thought hard for a minute. Then she took another bite of her veggie pitta roll.

I have no choice, she decided. *I have to ask him. I have to find out the truth.*

Mary-Kate finished eating her lunch. Then she wiped her mouth and stood up. She dropped her trash in the can and marched straight over to Pokey.

"Pokey, can I talk to you a minute?" she asked him.

He was seated with three other friends from class. All boys.

"Hi, Mary-Kate," one of the guys said.

"Hi," she answered.

"What's up?" Pokey asked.

"Uh, I need to talk to you alone," Mary-Kate said.

"Whatever," Pokey said, standing up. He followed her out of the cafeteria, into the hall. "What's wrong?" he asked. "You look sick."

I feel sick! Mary-Kate thought. *How am I supposed to find out if he asked me out for a date, without sounding like a jerk?*

Brian was right. It could be humiliating.

Mary-Kate cleared her throat. Maybe there was a way to ask without actually asking.

"Uh, it's about Saturday," Mary-Kate began. "About coming over to play basketball. I was just sort of wondering . . . are you going to come over and pick me up? Or should I get my dad to bring me over?"

Because if it's a date, Mary-Kate thought, *you'll come pick me up. Right?*

Pokey shrugged. "Makes no difference to me," he said. "I mean, I can get my mom to drive if your dad can't bring you."

Hmmm, Mary-Kate thought. *That doesn't answer the question.*

"Well, do I need to wear anything special?" Mary-Kate asked.

Pokey frowned and looked confused. "What for?"

"I don't know," Mary-Kate stammered. "Are we going to do anything *else* – besides play basketball?"

Pokey gave her an awkward stare and shrugged again. "If you want," he said. "Whatever you want to do is fine with me."

This is so hard! Mary-Kate thought. *He doesn't see what I'm getting at. And I can't think of a good way to say it!*

"I've got to go," Pokey said. He started to back away. "You still look sick. Are you getting the flu or something?"

"No," Mary-Kate said.

"Okay. See you Saturday," Pokey said.

"Wait!" Mary-Kate called. "Is anyone else going to be there?"

Pokey walked back to Mary-Kate. He shook his head fast. "No way," he said. "I don't want anyone else to know about this, okay? I mean, let's just keep it a secret."

A secret? Mary-Kate thought. *It is a date! Brian and Max were right!*

She felt her face getting hot.

Just then the bell rang. Lunch was over.

"I've got to go," Pokey repeated, strolling away.

"See you Saturday. If you don't get sick by then."

Sick? By Saturday? Mary-Kate thought.

It won't take that long, she realised. Because she felt sick already! And she knew that if she went out with Pokey on Saturday, she'd be more than sick.

She'd be dead! Because Ashley would kill her!

I have to tell Ashley that Pokey asked me out, Mary-Kate decided. *Ashley has to know the truth about him. But how am I going to tell her?*

How?

CHAPTER TEN

"And here's *another* thing Pokey and I have in common!" Ashley announced to her sister.

The two girls were lounging in their bedroom late that afternoon. Mary-Kate was playing Gameboy. Ashley lay on her flower-print quilt, writing something in a notebook.

"Don't you want to know what it is?" Ashley prompted.

"Okay," Mary-Kate said. "*What* do you and Pokey have in common?"

"Both our names end in E-Y!" Ashley gushed.

Oh, man, Mary-Kate thought. *How am I going to tell her the truth now? About Pokey asking me out? She's getting more and more of a crush on him!*

"Uh, you know, Ashley," Mary-Kate cautioned, "I wouldn't get too carried away with him. I mean, maybe you should take things slow."

Ashley tossed her blonde hair over her shoulder with a flick of her hand.

"Oh, I think I'm probably mature enough not to rush into anything," she informed Mary-Kate coolly.

Then she whirled around and quickly showed her sister the notebook she'd been writing in. "Which looks better? Ashley Valentine? Or Ashley Burke-Valentine?"

Mary-Kate rolled her eyes. "Marriage?" she exclaimed. "You're already planning to marry him?"

"Well, it wasn't my idea," Ashley argued. "We were talking about weird names the other day, and he said, 'Try living with Pokey for a while'. "

"So?" Mary-Kate asked.

"So think about it, Mary-Kate!" Ashley cried. "He asked me to try *living* with his name! Doesn't that sound like a proposal of marriage to you?"

"Not exactly." Mary-Kate shook her head.

Especially not when he's asked me *out for a date!* she thought.

Mary-Kate's throat closed up. Her stomach

turned over. She felt worse and worse.

Ashley was going to be so upset!

I've got to find some way to tell her, Mary-Kate decided.

But before Mary-Kate thought of a way to bring it up, Carrie poked her head into the twins' room. "It's your turn to set the table, Ashley," Carrie announced.

Ashley hopped up right away.

"My pleasure," she chirped. "Isn't life glorious?"

For you, maybe, Mary-Kate thought glumly. *For me, it's the pits!*

"Boy, she's in a good mood," Carrie commented when Ashley was gone.

"Not for long," Mary-Kate muttered.

"Oh – you saw dinner, huh?" Carrie guessed. "I swear it looked better on the box!"

"I'm not talking about dinner," Mary-Kate said. "It's . . . " She trailed off.

Carrie sat down on Mary-Kate's bed. "What's the matter?" she asked.

"I've got a problem," Mary-Kate admitted. "A big problem. About Ashley."

Carrie smiled.

"Oh, I get it," she said. "You're probably feeling a little jealous because Ashley might have a boyfriend. But don't worry – your time will come."

"It already has!" Mary-Kate blurted out.

"Really? Who is he?" Carrie scooted in closer to hear the news.

Mary-Kate gulped. "Pokey."

"Pokey?" Carrie's eyes opened wide. "Ashley's Pokey?"

Mary-Kate slapped the bed in frustration.

"How many Pokeys do you know?" she cried. "Yes, Ashley's Pokey! He invited me over to his house for a date. To play basketball! What am I going to do?"

"I think you *know* what you have to do," Carrie said. "You have to tell Ashley."

Mary-Kate's shoulders slumped. Sure, she *did* know that. But it was going to be hard. So hard.

"Can I do it from the pay phone on the corner?" Mary-Kate asked. "I mean, Ashley's scrawny – but she's got a great left hook!"

Carrie laughed and put her arm around Mary-Kate's shoulder.

"Just do it," Carrie advised. "The sooner the better."

Oh, boy, Mary-Kate thought. Her stomach turned again.

She knew she had to do it – just tell Ashley the

truth and get it over with.

But what she *didn't* know was this:

How mad was Ashley going to be when she found out?

CHAPTER
ELEVEN

"Professor! I have to talk to you right now!" Carrie exclaimed angrily the next morning.

Kevin Burke had been writing on the blackboard in his classroom. He put down his chalk and brushed his hands off in the air.

"Carrie," he said, greeting her. "You're early. Class doesn't begin until ten o'clock . . . tomorrow morning!"

Carrie put her hands on her hips. "Don't you dare try to change the subject!" she shot back. "I mean, how could you? How could you do it?"

Kevin walked across the room and quietly closed his classroom door. If she was going to shout, he didn't want the entire campus to hear it!

"This is about Rick, isn't it?" he asked.

"Yes!" Carrie snapped. "You failed him just to put him in his place, didn't you?"

Kevin shook his head.

"I'm sorry, Carrie," he told her, "but I can't discuss another student's grades."

Carrie narrowed her eyes.

"Oh, that's just a lame excuse," she said. "You don't want to admit the truth, but I know the truth. I read Rick's paper – and I know good work when I see it."

"Oh, it was good work," Kevin agreed. "No doubt about that. It was clear, concise, and the research was excellent."

Carrie stared at him, puzzled.

"I thought you couldn't talk about another student's work," she said.

But that's just the point, Kevin thought. *Don't you get it?*

"But I'm *not* talking about Rick's work," he explained.

"Then what *are* you talking about?" Carrie demanded.

Kevin let out a sigh. How could he explain it – without explaining it? There was no way.

Finally he gave in.

He reached into his briefcase and took out the old textbook that Rick had copied his research paper from.

"I'm talking about this," he said, handing her the book.

Kevin flipped the book open to a page he had marked.

"Start reading at the second paragraph," he told Carrie. He placed the book in her hands. "I think you'll see what I mean."

Carrie read silently for a minute. So silently that Kevin wondered if she'd stopped breathing. He could see from the frozen expression on her face that she was beginning to understand.

Carrie finally looked up.

"This is Rick's paper," she mumbled.

"And I can't figure out how it got into that book ten years before Rick wrote it!" Kevin said, making a halfhearted attempt at a joke.

Poor Carrie, he thought. He hated to burst her bubble, but she had to find out the truth some time. Better sooner than later, after all.

"He copied it?" Carrie sounded as if she still couldn't believe it.

"That's what I'd say if I could talk about it," Kevin answered. "But of course, I can't."

"But he said he worked so *hard* on his paper!" Carrie went on. "He even bragged about how many hours he spent in the library doing research. And how many books he had read."

"Well, it probably took him a while to find the right book to steal from," Kevin quipped.

Carrie was quiet – for practically the first time since Kevin had known her!

Finally, in a soft voice, she said, "I'm such a fool."

"No, you're not," Kevin comforted her. "Give yourself a break. Rick comes off like a really bright guy. And that can be really attractive."

"Oh, it's not that," Carrie scoffed. "I know tons of bright guys."

"Well, if it's not that he's smart, then what is it?" Kevin asked, really curious. "What made you like him?"

Carrie eyed Kevin sideways.

"If I tell you, can you keep a secret?" she asked shyly.

"Sure," he agreed. "Of course I can keep a secret. What is it?"

"It's his chin." Carrie blushed. "That's why I fell for him in the first place."

"His what?" Kevin blinked.

"His chin!" she repeated. "He's got one of those

strong chins, like George Clooney. I see one of those, and I just melt. It's my weakness."

Without meaning to, Kevin reached up and felt his own chin. It wasn't a wimpy chin – but it didn't look like it was carved out of stone, either.

He yanked his hand away quickly.

"Well, I know just how you feel," he said. "We all have a weakness for something. Something we're really attracted to."

Carrie's face lit up.

"Oh, really?" she said. She sounded interested. "What's your weakness?"

"Legs," Kevin admitted. "I like a woman with nice legs."

Carrie's eyes sparkled.

"I know the perfect woman for you!" she announced.

She started fishing around in her purse for a pen and piece of paper.

"Oh, no – " Kevin started to say.

But Carrie was on a roll. Totally excited. And Kevin knew better than to try to stop her when she got like that.

"Brooke!" Carrie announced, writing a name and phone number on a piece of paper. "You have to meet her. She's a friend of mine, and she has the greatest legs!"

"I thought we were going to stay out of each other's personal lives," Kevin argued.

"We are." Carrie nodded.

She put the piece of paper on his desk. "I'm just giving you her phone number," she said, "and you can do whatever you want with it."

Then she started heading for the door.

"Right," Kevin agreed. But he didn't want her to walk out quite yet. "Hey," he called. "You going to be okay?"

"Okay?" Carrie asked. "You mean about Rick?"

Kevin nodded. He really was sorry about this whole thing. He hated being the one to tell Carrie that Rick was a cheat and a fake in the 'smarts' department.

Carrie's face got sort of sad for a minute. But then she smiled.

"Yeah, I'll be fine," she said. "It's nothing that a hot bath and a pint of ice cream won't cure!"

"A whole pint, huh?" Kevin said with a laugh. "I'll have to remember that."

When she was gone, Kevin picked up the scrap of paper from the desk and pulled out a pen. Next to Brooke's name he wrote two words: GREAT LEGS.

Who knows? Kevin thought as he stuck the paper in his jeans pocket. Maybe he'd give her a call . . . someday.

If it didn't work out, he could always stock up on ice cream!

CHAPTER TWELVE

"Hey, Ashley, can I talk to you?" Mary-Kate asked as she hurried into the living room. Then she gazed at the coffee table and realised what Ashley was doing – laying out the paintbrushes and supplies for the history project.

Uh-oh, Mary-Kate thought. *Pokey's on his way!*

"Not now," Ashley answered. "I want to be sure everything is just right. Could you hand me that cushion?"

"This?" Mary-Kate tossed her a throw cushion from the couch. "What for?"

"I'm putting it on the floor so Pokey can kneel on it while we paint," Ashley explained. "Last time his knees got sore."

"Oh, poor baby," Mary-Kate muttered. "Listen, Ash, I've really got to talk to you before lover boy shows up."

Ashley put her hands on her hips and glared.

"I don't understand why you have to be so nasty about Pokey," she complained to her sister. "Or why you don't like him."

"Well, you will in a minute," Mary-Kate replied. "Look, there's no other way to tell you – so I'll just spit it out. The other day Pokey asked me out on a date."

"Yeah, right," Ashley shot back. "On what planet?"

"I'm serious. He did it while you were making him a smoothie," Mary-Kate insisted.

Ashley stared at her sister for a moment.

"You're lying," she finally said.

Mary-Kate shook her head solemnly. "No, I'm not," she said. "Why would I lie?"

"Because I have a boyfriend and you don't!" Ashley guessed. "You're jealous."

Mary-Kate rolled her eyes. This was hard. How could she convince Ashley of the truth – without hurting her feelings even more?

"Look, if you don't believe me, ask Max and Brian," Mary-Kate finally said. "They were here."

Ashley's face fell. Her voice cracked. "He asked you out *in front* of them?"

Mary-Kate nodded. "Pretty lame, huh?" she said softly.

"But why? Why would he do that?" Ashley asked. She sounded totally miserable.

"Because he's a jerk!" Mary-Kate announced.

Mary-Kate watched her sister's face droop lower and lower. It made her feel horrible to hit her twin with this news. But someone had to tell her the truth.

"Pokey will be here any minute," Ashley moaned. "How can I face him? What should I do?"

Mary-Kate thought for a minute. Maybe there was a way to pay Pokey back for hurting Ashley.

"I say we mess with his head a little," Mary-Kate suggested, her eyes dancing.

"How?" Ashley asked.

"Fuss over him," Mary-Kate said. "Treat him like a prince. Make him think he's got two girls – not just one – hanging on his every royal word. And then we yank the throne out from under him!"

"I like it!" Ashley said, nodding.

An instant later the doorbell rang.

"Okay, let me handle this," Ashley declared. She flung open the door.

Pokey Valentine stood there grinning. He flicked his light brown hair off his forehead, pushing it away from his eyes.

"Hi, Ashley," he said.

Ashley turned on the charm. "Pokey! Come in, come in," she gushed. She led him into the living room, gesturing toward Mary-Kate along the way. "I believe you know Mary-Kate."

Mary-Kate copied her sister's fake-friendly voice exactly. "Hello, Pokey," she said.

Pokey looked confused.

"Sit down," Ashley cooed. She practically forced him on to the couch. Then both girls sat down, one on either side of him.

Ashley grabbed the cushion from the floor and placed it behind his head. Mary-Kate fluffed it for him.

"Comfy?" Mary-Kate asked, leaning close to him.

Pokey squirmed. "Uh . . . yeah," he managed to say.

"Can I get you anything?" Ashley asked in a supersweet voice. "A soda? A smoothie? Or . . . " Her voice became angry. "My sister?"

Pokey leaped off the couch.

"What's with you guys?" he asked, backing away.

Ashley stood up, too. She planted her hands on her hips.

"Mary-Kate says you asked her out on a date!" Ashley accused him.

"What? No way!" Pokey replied.

"Come on, Pokey," Mary-Kate joined in. "Admit it. You asked me to come over for Saturday – to play basketball 'and stuff'."

Pokey shrugged. "That's because you've got a great jump shot," he explained. "I figured maybe you could help me with mine."

Mary-Kate glared. "Oh, yeah? What about telling me to keep it a secret?"

"I didn't want the guys to find out you were coaching me," Pokey admitted. "I mean, it's bad enough having a girl help me with basketball. I didn't want anyone to know about it."

Mary-Kate threw up her arms. "Well, what about the 'and stuff' part?" she demanded.

"The 'and stuff' part?" Pokey repeated. He looked totally confused.

"Yes!" Mary-Kate practically shouted. "Brian and Max were here! They heard you say it! You asked me to come over to play basketball 'and stuff.' What was the 'and stuff' part, if it wasn't a date?"

"Well, my dribbling's bad, too," Pokey admitted sheepishly.

Oh, man, Mary-Kate thought. *This is so embarrassing. I accused him of asking me out – only he didn't! And I got Ashley upset over nothing!*

Why did I ever listen to Max and Brian?

"So it wasn't a date?" Mary-Kate asked, just to be sure.

"No!" Pokey blurted out. "Why would I ask you out when I like Ashley?"

Whoa! Mary-Kate thought. *Did he just say – out loud – what I thought he said?*

She glanced at her sister. Ashley's eyes were wide with surprise.

"You like me?" Ashley asked.

"Well . . . I guess. Kind of," Pokey admitted.

A huge smile spread over Ashley's face.

"Good!" she announced happily. "Because I kind of like you, too!"

All right! Mary-Kate thought, breathing a sigh of relief. "And *no one* kind of likes me!" she cried cheerfully. "Life is good!"

Pokey and Ashley laughed.

Life is good – except for one thing, Mary-Kate realised. She grabbed her coat and headed for the door.

It was payback time.

"Where are you going?" Ashley asked.

"To see Max and Brian," Mary-Kate replied.

"Uh-oh," Ashley said. "What are you going to do?"

"Hurt them . . . and stuff!" Mary-Kate announced.

CHAPTER THIRTEEN

"Well, what's your favourite fraction?" Ashley asked Pokey. She lay back on her bed later that night, talking into the phone.

"His favourite fraction?" Mary-Kate repeated from her side of the room. "I don't believe this! You've been on the phone for two hours! And now you're talking about fractions?"

"Well, I couldn't think of anything else!" Ashley whispered, covering the phone for a moment. "I mean, I've got his favourite colour, food, song, movie, and day of the week all memorised! What more is there?"

"How about his favourite number of hours to *sleep* each night!" Mary-Kate suggested. "Come on,

Ash. It's late and I'm totally beat."

Ashley turned back to the phone. "I've got to go, Pokey," she informed him.

"Okay, but you hang up first," he said.

"No, you first," Ashley said.

"No, you hang up first," Pokey said.

"No, you hang up," Ashley begged him.

Mary-Kate rolled her eyes and jumped out of bed. She marched over to Ashley's side of the room and grabbed the phone.

"Here's an idea," she snapped. "*I'll* hang up first!"

Beep. She pushed the button and disconnected the call.

"Thanks, Mary-Kate," Ashley said gratefully. "I was beginning to run out of things to say!"

"Really?" Mary-Kate cracked. "I thought your twenty-minute conversation on why cheese smells was fascinating!"

Ashley put the phone on her dresser just as her dad popped into the twins' bedroom.

"Hey, you two," he greeted them. "It's getting late. Shouldn't the lights be out already?"

"Yes!" Mary-Kate agreed quickly.

"Hold on," Kevin said. "You went along with that too fast. What am I missing? Have you washed

74

your face yet? Or brushed your teeth?"

Mary-Kate didn't answer. Instead she jumped into bed and slid down deeper under the covers.

"Mary-Kate?" he asked, his eyes drilling into her. "Come on . . . "

"I chewed some Dentyne after lunch," she mumbled from under the duvet. "Does that count?"

"Nope," Kevin answered. He pointed towards the bathroom. "Go. Brush."

Mary-Kate groaned.

She dragged herself out of bed one more time and shuffled off towards the bathroom, leaving Ashley and their dad alone.

Kevin stood up and moved over to Ashley's bed. He sat down beside her.

"So, Ashley, is everything okay with you and Pokey?" he asked.

Uh-oh, Ashley thought. *Time for one of Dad's heart-to-heart talks.*

She knew the minute her dad started asking questions in that 'just making conversation' tone of voice that he was trying to pry information out of her!

And there was no way she was going to let him do that.

After all, her boyfriends were her own private business and nobody else's. Right?

On the other hand, she didn't want to come right to the point and tell him to butt out. His feelings would be hurt.

"Pokey?" she repeated. "Uh, sure, Dad. Everything's fine."

"He seems like a pretty neat kid," Kevin added.

"Yeah, I guess so," she said.

"So, you want to tell me a little about him?" Kevin asked.

"No, thanks, Dad. That's okay."

"Are you sure?" he asked gently. "Because I want you to know it's okay for us to talk about special people in our lives. Like boys. After all, I am one, and I know all the secrets. And I don't mind sharing them with you."

"I'll keep that in mind," she said.

Mary-Kate padded back into the room a moment later. She opened her mouth, displaying her brushed teeth.

"There," she announced to her dad. "Are you happy?"

"Ecstatic," Kevin said.

"Listen, uh, Dad," Mary-Kate said. "I couldn't help hearing what you were just telling Ashley. You know, about how we should be able to talk about special people in our lives."

"Oh, good!" Kevin nodded. "I'm glad you heard that too, Mary-Kate. Of course, if you have someone you'd like to discuss . . . "

"Well," Mary-Kate said, winking at Ashley. "Do you really mean it? We can really talk to you about anybody?"

"Absolutely!" Kevin said quickly. "Any time somebody new comes into our lives, we should be comfortable enough to share it with each other."

"Great!" Mary-Kate said. Then she trotted over to her dresser, picked up a piece of paper, and waved it at her dad. "So who's Brooke?" she demanded.

Kevin's face turned bright red. He stared at the paper as if he didn't want to touch it.

"Where'd you get that?" he asked.

"Laundry-room floor," Mary-Kate replied as she passed the slip of paper over for Ashley to see. "We already know she has great legs. Anything else you want to tell us?"

Kevin reached out to grab the paper from Ashley. But Ashley yanked it away fast and held it out of reach.

"Come on, Dad," Ashley teased him. "You know

you can tell us anything. And we are girls, so we know all the secrets."

"And we'd be happy to share them with you," Mary-Kate joined in.

"I'd say you know *one too many* secrets!" Kevin said.

He reached out and tried to grab the paper away from Ashley again.

But Ashley crumpled it up and tossed it over his head to Mary-Kate.

"Mary-Kate! Give that to me!" he called, trying to sound firm.

He lunged for the paper, but Mary-Kate threw it back to her sister's side of the room.

"All right," Kevin announced, standing up. "I give up! I can see I'm in over my head. It's time for bed, anyway."

He flipped off the light and started out of the room.

Both girls giggled.

"Are you sure you don't want to *share* this with us, Dad?" Mary-Kate teased.

Kevin paused for a moment in the dark. "Uh, no," he said. "Goodnight."

Phew, Ashley thought. *Close one!* She wasn't sure she really wanted to know who Brooke was anyway!

"Goodnight, Dad," Mary-Kate called in the dark.

"Goodnight," he said again as he headed down the stairs.

CHAPTER
FOURTEEN

Mary-Kate crawled into her bed and pulled up the covers. Her bed felt cosy. And she was definitely ready for sleep.

All this stuff about boyfriends – and dates – had made her totally nervous and tired. Especially when she thought Ashley might be mad at her! That would have been the worst.

She couldn't stand it if a boy ever came between them.

And maybe, someday, a boy would.

Mary-Kate swallowed hard, pushing the idea back down. *Don't think about it,* she told herself.

At least for now, things were back to normal. And normal meant that all she should be worrying about was her lay-up shot!

"Mary-Kate?" Ashley called from her side of the room.

"Yeah?" Mary-Kate answered from under the covers.

"I've been thinking," Ashley began. "And I want you to know that even though I have a boyfriend now, I don't want anything to change between us. Ever."

Me either, Mary-Kate thought.

"But it will," she answered a moment later.

"How?" Ashley asked.

"Now, when I'm trying to fall asleep, you won't be talking about clothes all night," Mary-Kate predicted. "Or make-up. You'll be talking about Pokey!"

Ashley giggled.

"But honestly, Mary-Kate," she went on. "I just want you to know that whatever goes on between me and Pokey – it won't affect us, okay? You're my sister and my best friend. You always will be."

Ashley paused. "And no boy is ever going to change that. You know what I mean?"

Mary-Kate was quiet for a moment.

Then, from under the covers, she called, "Ashley?"

"Yes?"

"Thanks," Mary-Kate said. "And you know what?"

"What?" Ashley answered.

"The same goes for me, too. I'll never let a boy come between us either," Mary-Kate offered. "Unless . . . "

"Unless what?" Ashley demanded.

Mary-Kate pulled the covers completely over her head before answering. Just in case a pillow came flying at her.

"Unless he has a jump shot better than Shaq's!" Mary-Kate joked.

Pow! The pillow landed with a thud on Mary-Kate's head.

But she didn't care. She was completely happy. Everything was great between her and Ashley. And that's all that really mattered.

Mary-Kate left the pillow right where it was. Then she smiled to herself and snuggled down into her bed.

Besides, she thought as she drifted off to sleep. *No one had a jump shot better than Shaq's!*

And that meant that no one was likely to come between the twins for a very, very long time.

Mary-Kate & Ashley's Scrapbook

Once upon a time . . .
we were just two sisters . . .
dreaming about boys but never dating them.

Then Ashley got
her first crush - on
a boy called Pokey
Valentine.

She spent a lot of time talking to him on the phone.

Sure, I knew how much Ashley liked Pokey. And I'm not interested in any boy - not yet, anyway. But then Pokey asked *me* out on a date instead of Ashley - at least, I thought he did. I had no clue what to do. So I asked Carrie - and she said I'd better tell Ashley the bad news.

Ashley *hated* what I had to say.

She even got sort of mad...

Then it turned
out that Pokey
really liked
Ashley, not me!
Life is good...

So now everything is
back to normal...
until the next boy
comes along!

PSST! Take a sneak peak
at

To Snoop or Not to Snoop?

"There they are!" Ellen Mitnick pointed a finger at Mary-Kate and Ashley Burke. "They're the ones who have been snooping on us! With a telescope!"

Mary-Kate and Ashley stood on the stoop in front of their house. Their father, Kevin, stood next to them. They were surrounded by a crowd of angry kids.

"They said I throw the newspapers into the bushes," Victor Nunzio, the Penny Pincher delivery boy said. "But I didn't mean to. Dearborn Street is just a very windy block!"

"And they said a cable guy was breaking into our house!" ten-year-old Scott Pack said. "They scared him away and I missed the Cubs game!"

Mary-Kate could feel her face turn red. *Whoops.*

"And my dad does not clip his nosehairs over the sink!" a girl with glasses declared.

Kevin Burke looked stern. He turned to the twins. "Well, girls, what do you have to say for yourself?"

Mary-Kate had a sinking feeling in her stomach. *We're in trouble now*, she thought. *Help me out here, Ashley!*

"We were just keeping an eye on Dearborn Street!" Ashley explained. "We were just trying to help!"

"Well, you'd better stop," Scott said. "Because we're all fed up with it!"

The kids filed down the steps and marched past Mary-Kate and Ashley. When the kids were down the block, the twins turned slowly to their father.

"So that's what you've been doing up in the attic with the telescope," Kevin said. "I thought you were exploring the solar system – not the whole neighbourhood!"

"Dad," Mary-Kate said. "We can explain."

"We were just looking out for trouble," Ashley explained. "Every street needs someone to watch over it."

Kevin shook his head. "My own two daughters – snoopers!"

"But Dad, we're not just snoopers!" Ashley cried.

"We're Super Snoopers!" Mary-Kate said proudly.

"And you'll be in super trouble if you try it

again, "Kevin said. "From now on there'll be no more snooping. Ever!"

As Kevin walked back into the house, the twins stared at each other.

"No more snooping?" Mary-Kate wailed. "What will we do now?"

"There's always homework," Ashley suggested.

She and Mary-Kate opened the door and went back inside. Slowly they trudged up the stairs to the attic.

"Homework – now there's a concept," Mary-Kate grumbled. What was due tomorrow? she wondered. Maths? History? She'd rather find out about people living today than about someone who died hundreds of years ago!

The twins entered the attic. Mary-Kate leaned on the telescope. It was pointed directly out the attic window on to the street. She could see the lights on in Mrs. Baker's house. Mrs. Baker used to babysit for Mary-Kate and Ashley, before their new babysitter, Carrie, arrived. Mrs. Baker was nice, but she was old and fussy. She used to make the twins wear sweaters just because *she* was cold!

Mary-Kate could see Mrs. Baker and her boyfriend, Mr. Fillmore, standing in front of the living-room window.

"It's date night at Mrs. Baker's," Mary-Kate sighed. "I don't need a telescope to tell me that."

She was about to turn away when she saw something else. Mr. Fillmore was waving two pointed objects at Mrs. Baker. They looked like knitting needles!

"Hey," Mary-Kate said. "There's something going on at Mrs. Baker's house. Check it out."

Ashley shook her head. "Mary-Kate!" she cried. "I can't believe you're snooping after what Dad said!"

"I'm just being a good neighbour!" Mary-Kate said. She sat down behind the telescope and adjusted the focus. "If we don't keep an eye on Dearborn Street, who will?"

"It looks like Mrs. Baker and Mr. Fillmore are having a fight!" Mary-Kate said.

Ashley stared at Mary-Kate.

"Go ahead," Ashley said. She paced the attic nervously. "You can snoop if you want to. But I'm keeping my promise!"

"Suit yourself," Mary-Kate said. Her eyes opened wide. "But now – Mrs. Baker has picked up a huge knife!"

"A knife?" Ashley shrieked. She shoved Mary-Kate off of the chair. "Give me that thing!"

Ashley pressed her eye against the telescope. "You're right!" she exclaimed. "Mrs. Baker is waving a knife at Mr. Fillmore!"

"Wow!" she said. "I wonder why they could be fighting."

"I'll bet it's because of that other woman Mrs. Baker was talking about. Mr. Fillmore must be seeing her too!" Mary-Kate declared.

"But he's so old!" Ashley exclaimed. "He must be at least seventy. How does he have the energy to date two people at the same time?"

"Let me see again," Mary-Kate said. She took the telescope from Ashley and steadied it.

"Mrs. Baker is pulling down the shade," Mary-Kate said in a hushed voice. "But I can still see her shadow."

Suddenly she gasped. "Ashley! She's raising her knife in the air. Oh, no! Mr. Fillmore has disappeared!"

Mary-Kate spun around and stared at Ashley. "His shadow has slipped right off the shade! Do you know what that means?"

"No, what?" Ashley asked.

"I think Mr. Fillmore is gone for good," Mary-Kate said slowly. "I think Mrs. Baker's killed him!"

Ashley stared at her sister.

"You're losing it, Mary-Kate," Ashley said. "Mrs. Baker may be cold all the time, but she's not a cold-blooded murderer. There's got to be a good explanation."

"Think about it, Ashley," Mary-Kate said. She looked up from the telescope. "Mr. Fillmore is seeing another woman, right? And Mrs. Baker said it made her so mad that she could kill him."

"It's just an expression," Ashley said. "Besides, there's absolutely no way Mrs. Baker could stab Mr. Fillmore!"

"Why not?" Mary-Kate asked.

"Because she has arthritis!" Ashley insisted. "She can't even slice a pound cake!"

Mary-Kate paced the attic. "We have to blow the whistle on Mrs. Baker," she said. "We have to tell Dad."

"Dad?" Ashley shrieked. "If he finds out we were snooping again, he'll freak."

"He'll freak if he finds out we saw a crime committed and we didn't tell him," Mary-Kate pointed out.

Ashley rolled her eyes. There was no talking Mary-Kate out of this one!

"Dad won't be home until late tonight," Ashley said. "He said he has a meeting, remember?"

"Then we'll tell Carrie instead," Mary-Kate said. *Someone* has to know."

"Know what?" Carrie asked. She poked her head in the attic door.

Ashley gulped. "Mary-Kate thinks— "

"I think I saw Mrs. Baker kill Mr. Fillmore," Mary-Kate interrupted. She described the scene in Mrs. Baker's house.

Carrie stared in disbelief. "Mrs. Baker wouldn't hurt a fly," she said. She began to laugh. "That's one of the silliest ideas I've ever heard!"

"Now come on down and get some dinner," she said. "And stay away from that telescope!"

"Now are you satisfied?" Ashley asked when Carrie had gone.

"I'm still going to tell Dad," Mary-Kate insisted. "I'll stay up all night if I have to – until he comes home!"

"Fine!" Ashley said. "But you're totally wrong about Mrs. Baker. You've been reading too many murder mysteries."

Mary-Kate stared out the window.

"I hope you're right, Ashley. But I know what I saw – and it doesn't look good!"

to be continued...

mary-kateandashley

TWO of a kind ™

Coming soon – can you collect them all?

(1) It's a Twin Thing   (0 00 714480 6)

(2) How to Flunk Your First Date   (0 00 714479 2)

(3) The Sleepover Secret   (0 00 714478 4)

(4) One Twin Too Many   (0 00 714477 6)

(5) To Snoop or Not to Snoop   (0 00 714476 8)

(6) My Sister the Supermodel   (0 00 714475 X)

(7) Two's a Crowd   (0 00 714474 1)

(8) Let's Party   (0 00 714473 3)

(9) Calling All Boys   (0 00 714472 5)

(10) Winner Take All   (0 00 714471 7)

(11) PS Wish You Were Here   (0 00 714470 9)

(12) The Cool Club   (0 00 714469 5)

(13) War of the Wardrobes   (0 00 714468 7)

(14) Bye-Bye Boyfriend   (0 00 714467 9)

(15) It's Snow Problem   (0 00 714466 0)

(16) Likes Me, Likes Me Not   (0 00 714465 2)

(17) Shore Thing   (0 00 714464 4)

(18) Two for the Road   (0 00 714463 6)

HarperCollins*Entertainment*

mary-kateandashley

Meet Chloe and Riley Carlson.
So much to do...

so little time

(1)	How to Train a Boy	(0 00 714458 X)
(2)	Instant Boyfriend	(0 00 714448 2)
(3)	Too Good to be True	(0 00 714449 0)
(4)	Just Between Us	(0 00 714450 4)
(5)	Tell Me About It	(0 00 714451 2)
(6)	Secret Crush	(0 00 714452 0)

*... and more
to come!*

HarperCollins*Entertainment*

 PARACHUTE PRESS

DUALSTAR PUBLICATIONS

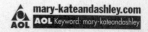 mary-kateandashley.com
AOL Keyword: mary-kateandashley

TM & © 2002 Dualstar Entertainment Group, Inc.

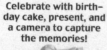

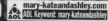

Order Form

To order direct from the publishers, just make a list of the titles you want and fill in the form below:

Name ....

Address ....

....

....

Send to: Dept 6, HarperCollins Publishers Ltd, Westerhill Road, Bishopbriggs, Glasgow G64 2QT.

Please enclose a cheque or postal order to the value of the cover price, plus:

UK & BFPO: Add £1.00 for the first book, and 25p per copy for each additional book ordered.

Overseas and Eire: Add £2.95 service charge. Books will be sent by surface mail but quotes for airmail despatch will be given on request.

A 24-hour telephone ordering service is available to holders of Visa, MasterCard, Amex or Switch cards on 0141- 772 2281.

Collins
An *Imprint of* HarperCollins*Publishers*